This book has been specially written and published for World Book Day 2014. For further information, visit **www.worldbookday.com**

World Book Day in the UK and Ireland is made possible by generous sponsorship from National Book Tokens, participating publishers, authors and booksellers.

Booksellers who accept the £1/€1.50 World Book Day Book Token bear the full cost of redeeming it.

World Book Day, **World Book Night** and **Quick Reads** are annual initiatives designed to encourage everyone in the UK and Ireland — whatever your age — to read more and discover the joy of books.

World Book Night is a celebration of books and reading for adults and teens on 23 April, which sees book gifting and celebrations in thousands of communities around the country: **www.worldbooknight.org**

Quick Reads provides brilliant short new books by bestselling authors to engage adults in reading: **www.quickreads.org.uk**

D1102503

Mary Arrigan studied at the National College of Art, Dublin, and at Florence University. She became a fulltime writer in 1994. Her novel for teenagers, *The Rabbit Girl*, one of her forty-two published books, was selected by The United States Board of Books for Young People on their list of Outstanding International Books for 2012. Her awards include the International White Ravens title, a Bisto Merit Award, *The Sunday Times* Crime Writers Association Award and The Hennessy Short Story Award. Her books have been translated into twelve languages. You can read more Milo Adventures in *Milo and One Dead Angry Druid*, and *Milo and the Long Lost Warriors*.

THE MILO ADVENTURES

MILO AND THE LONG LOST WARRIORS

WRITTEN AND ILLUSTRATED BY

MARY ARRIGAN

THE O'BRIEN PRESS
DUBLIN

First published 2014 by The O'Brien Press Ltd.,
12 Terenure Road East, Rathgar, Dublin 6, Ireland.
Tel: +353 1 4923333; Fax: +353 1 4922777
E-mail: books@obrien.ie
Website: www.obrien.ie

ISBN: 978-1-84717-633-2

1 2 3 4 5 6 7 8 9 10
14 15 16 17 18

Layout and design: The O'Brien Press Ltd.
Cover illustrations: Neil Price
Printed and bound by CPI Group (UK) Ltd, Croydon, CR0 4YY

The paper in this book is produced using pulp from
managed forests.

The O'Brien Press receives assistance from

For David, Michael and Joanna

CONTENTS

CHAPTER ONE

MISS LEE'S SURPRISE

When Miss Lee announced that we were going on a school trip to Dublinia, there was a hush of disbelief. Only for three seconds, of course, because when her words reached our brains we all whooped and whistled at the thoughts of a train journey and a day off school.

Except Shane.

'You mean *Dublin,* miss,' he said. 'There's no "inia" at the end of it.'

'It's a special museum,' I told him.

'Museum!' he practically exploded. 'They're all the same – skulls with bad teeth and shelves full of cracked pots – I've seen the pictures on Google. You can count me out, Miss.'

Miss Lee laughed and explained that Dublinia is a brilliant place that shows what Ireland and its people were like long ago in the middle ages.

'Every room and every character look so real, you'll think you're part of ancient times,' she said. 'It's so good you won't want to leave. Besides,' she added, 'after that we'll be going to see a re-enactment of the Battle of Clontarf.'

'Really?' said Shane.

'Really and truly, Shane,' said Miss Lee.

'Well, that's OK then,' Shane muttered. 'I'll go then.'

On our way home from school Shane and I were like a pair of chatty magpies going on and on about the trip. Shane had never even been to Dublin, never mind the Dublinia museum. He and his gran, Big Ella, came from Africa to live in Ireland when he was little. They live on the same road as me, and Shane is my best mate.

'Coffee and cream,' Big Ella calls us because of our different skin colours.

We were chattering away, wheeling our bikes, when we heard rough accents we didn't want to hear.

'Well, well,' sniggered a familiar voice from behind. 'What has you nerds so chatty?'

'Yeah, share it with us,' put in the other voice we didn't want to hear.

They were Wedge and Crunch, our arch enemies from sixth class – whenever they come to school, that is.

'You guys sound real chirpy,' said Wedge. 'Share it with us, won't ya?'

We both tried to mount our bikes. Big mistake.

'Ah, come on now,' said Crunch,

grabbing my carrier and knocking off my schoolbag. 'It's rude to run from friends.'

'Yeah,' added Wedge, pushing over Shane's bike. 'Let's join the conversation. Me and Crunch like a bit of conversation. Isn't that so, Crunch?'

'Yeah, we love a nice chat, we do.' Crunch laughed as he kicked Shane's schoolbag, sending his books all over the pavement. 'So, what has you two girlies so excited?'

'School,' I mumbled.

'School?' yelped Crunch, putting his hands over his ears. 'We're totally allergic to school. Come on, Wedge. We might catch some schooly germs from these two.'

'No,' said Wedge, who is the one with part of a brain. 'I think there's something more.'

Shane looked at me and shrugged his shoulders. Which meant it was up to me to take the flak, as usual.

'A school outing,' I muttered.

'A school outing!' whooped Crunch. 'How very jolly. Soggy sandwiches and paddling in the freezing sea – NOT! Come on, Wedge. I feel sick already.'

'Shut it, Crunch,' said Wedge, screwing his eyes and giving me a scary look. 'Even nerds don't get so excited about school stuff. So, come on, you two. Where's this outing going?'

'Dublin,' put in Shane.

'Ah, Dublin,' said Wedge. 'That's more

like our sort of thing, Crunch.'

'Yeah,' Crunch agreed. 'Dublin's OK. We can do stuff in Dublin, Wedge.'

'Thanks folks,' said Wedge. 'We'll put in a few days at school and get ourselves on that trip.'

Then they went off, whooping and laughing.

'Now look at what you've done,' muttered Shane as we gathered our books. 'They'll ruin everything.'

'What I'VE done?' I exclaimed. 'It was you who spilt the beans about Dublin. You could easily have said some boring gardens or an old church. Now we'll have those two breathing fire on us on the trip.'

CHAPTER TWO

MISTER LEWIS'S PLAN

At teatime, I spent most of the time shoving my favourite shepherd's pie around the plate with my fork.

'Not hungry, Milo?' asked Mum.

'Have I left something out of the ingredients?'

'Maybe the shepherd's toes,' said Dad, with a laugh. 'What's wrong, lad? Are you coming down with something – or is there a maths test tomorrow and you're not up for it?'

'No,' I said. 'It's the school outing.'

'Ah,' said Dad. 'Another trip to a town with falling arches, a sluggish river and a bird-pooed statue of someone nobody ever heard of.'

'No, Dad. It's the Dublinia museum.'

'Ah, sorry, son,' said Dad, patting my shoulder. 'I've been meaning to take you there …'

'No, it's not that,' I said. 'It's something else.'

'You don't want to go?' Mum asked.

'I do,' I said. 'I so want to go. Me and Shane are really dying to go.'

'His gran can't afford it?' Dad went on.

'Of course she can,' I said, making a volcano of shepherd's pie with my fork.

'Someone bothering you?' Dad asked softly as Mum went into the kitchen to turn off the scorching tart under the grill.

'Kinda,' I sighed.

'Want me to have a word?' he went on. 'I am a qualified policeman with full uniform and shiny handcuffs you know ...'

'NO!' I replied, knocking over my volcano. 'That'd be the worst thing ever.'

'Well,' said Dad, 'never forget that you are above whatever rubbish others get up to. Keep calm and stare them down, son.'

Yeah, that would really send Wedge and Crunch screaming down the street. As if!

Later on, I cycled to the town castle to meet up with my good, dead friend, Mister Lewis. Years and years ago he used to live in the house where Shane and Big Ella now live. He's now the resident ghost in the recently done-up castle in town. I went around to the portcullis at the front of the courtyard, thinking maybe he was doing a bit of scaring. He sometimes does that when he gets bored – giving the odd oOohhh at passersby from the high windows

'I have to get some bit of fun in the evenings, Milo,' he'd say to me, with an evil grin.

Sure enough he was sitting on a high-up windowsill, looking out for lone victims across the street. His face lit up when he saw me – insofar as a dead person's face can light up.

'Milo, my friend,' he said, wafting down beside me. 'Come, tell me all your news.'

I shrugged my shoulders. I hate when anyone asks me about 'news' because I never have any news worth telling. However, this time I had the museum trip to talk about.

'Museum,' he said, politely, but I

knew he wasn't impressed. After all, he had lived back when museum stuff was a normal part of his life. 'That's nice. Whereabouts is it?'

'Dublin,' I said.

'Dublin! Which museum?' he exclaimed, leaning closer.

'Dublinia,' I said.

'Dublinia!' he screeched, shaking his head like one of those loopy nodding dogs you see in the back of old cars. 'Really? The medieval Dublinia? Tell me, my boy,' he went on, staring at me so scarily that I figured his brain had finally shut down, 'what is the form of transport?'

'Train,' I said.

'Oh Milo, this is wonderful news.

Wonderful. You have no idea just how wonderful.' Now he was dancing on his skinny legs and waving his hands.

'Calm down, Mister Lewis,' I said as he bent towards me, his waxy-coloured nose almost touching my freckled one.

'Milo,' he said, 'there are three lost warriors, called Olaf, Gunnar and Alfred, trapped in that museum. They thought they were back in their own time; it's so realistic. For years and years I've been so frustrated that I couldn't help them from a distance. Now, I can come with you on the train and finally free them.'

The back of my neck chilled. 'Free them to do what exactly?' I asked.

'To join in their battle,' said Mister Lewis.

'What battle?'

'The Battle of Clontarf,' my spooky friend replied. 'If they don't get there, the whole history of Ireland will be changed.'

'Changed how, Mister Lewis?' I asked. 'How come it hasn't changed before now?'

'Because,' Mister Lewis whispered, 'this is the year 2014.'

'So?' I was still puzzled.

'The Battle of Clontarf was fought in 1014,' Mister Lewis said. 'One thousand years ago exactly. The magical time lapse that causes old enemies to rise again.'

CHAPTER THREE

A SCARE ON A TRAIN

In spite of the drizzly rain, the noise on the platform was mega as the kids from second class up to sixth were chattering and laughing like a bunch of hyenas. Not that I've ever heard a hyena, but Dad says it sounds like crooks when they're nicked for robbing.

'Wonderful, simply wonderful.'

I jumped when Mister Lewis whispered in my ear. I should be used to his trick of going invisible whenever he needs to, but it always freaks me out.

'What a wonderful, lively atmosphere, Milo,' he went on.

'Are you sure you're the only one who can get these guys out of the museum?' I whispered back.

'Absolutely,' he replied. 'Other – eh – spooks, as you call us, have tried throughout the ages, but I am a historian,' he said, proudly. 'And I'm well versed in the movements of the sun and moon ...'

'Was,' I said. 'You're dead, remember.'

'Who are you talking to, Milo?' asked Shane, shifting his big schoolbag on his shoulder. I knew it was full of Big Ella's excellent sandwiches and buns.

'He's talking to me, Shane, lad,' whispered Mister Lewis.

'Mister Lewis!' Shane exclaimed, looking around the crowded platform.

I had introduced him to Mister Lewis only two weeks ago when he followed me to the castle and thought I'd gone crazy talking to myself, so Mister Lewis had made himself visible and now the three of us are sound buddies.

'Ssshhh,' whispered Mister Lewis. 'I'm not showing myself just now.'

'Cool,' Mister Lewis.' Shane laughed. 'I wish I could do that.'

'Mmm. It has its advantages,' Mister Lewis said.

'Why won't you show yourself?' whispered Shane. 'Give the teachers a scare?'

'No, that won't be necessary,' Mister Lewis replied. 'I just want peace and a quiet nap. It's been many years since I travelled.'

There was a mad scramble for seats when the train pulled in. Shane and I got window seats across from one another.

'Where's Mister Lewis?' Shane asked, standing up and looking around as the train began to move.

27

'He'll be OK,' I said. 'He's pretty clever for an old dead guy.'

'I heard that' came a voice from overhead.

'You're up on the luggage rack?' Shane uttered. 'Wow, that's cool.'

'What's cool, pea-brain?' asked a gravelly voice that we knew well. My heart sank.

'Shouldn't you two be with sixth class?' I said, hoping I sounded tough, but knowing I sounded like a cat coughing up a furball.

'Ha!' laughed Wedge. 'Me and Crunch, we don't use the "*should*", word. That right, Crunch?'

'Yeah,' said Crunch. 'That's a word that *should* never be used.'

'So, shove over there, you two and make room,' ordered Wedge, giving Shane a poke that made his belly wobble.

As the train began to gather speed, we both pressed ourselves to the window to be as far away as possible from them. Shane lifted his bag to make more room.

'What's in the bag?' asked Wedge, who was sitting beside him.

'Nothing,' muttered Shane.

'A bag of nothing!' laughed Wedge. 'Let's have a look at your "nothing".'

As Wedge reached over to snatch the bag from Shane, a skinny arm with bony fingers dropped from overhead and swung gently above Crunch's head. Wedge's mouth dropped to his chest, and his eyes were like marbles on springs.

'What you lookin' at me like that for, Wedge?' Crunch whispered.

Wedge couldn't speak. He just kept staring at the freaky arm – with no body attached.

That's when Crunch looked up and saw the grey hand swinging over his head. His panicky shouts could be heard all over the carriage as he reached up and pulled the emergency cord.

When the train screeched to a halt, we sat back, me and Shane, and waited for the fun to start. Within seconds, the principal, Mrs Riley, marched up from one side of the carriage, the wispy moustache over her upper lip trembling with anger. The sixth-class teacher, Mister Brody, came from the other side, followed by the ticket collector.

Shane nudged me in the ribs. 'This is better than a movie, Milo.' He giggled as the interrogation began.

The more Wedge and Crunch went on and on about the dead arm, the redder and angrier the adults became. Mister Brody reached into the luggage rack and shook his head. Then Wedge pointed to Shane and me.

'Ask those two,' he whined. 'They saw it too.'

'Us?' said Shane, all innocence and disbelief. 'I didn't see anything strange. Did you see anything strange, Milo?'

I shrugged my shoulders. 'No, nothing

weird.'

Well, if you think about it, we weren't telling a lie – Mister Lewis is not weird as far as we're concerned. He's our friend and you don't call friends weird.

As the two of them were shunted off to be supervised for the rest of the journey, Wedge looked back and gave us the 'devil' sign with his fingers. We just smiled.

'Result, Mister Lewis,' Shane whispered up to the luggage rack.

'Result indeed, lad,' Mister Lewis whispered back.

I hoped so.

CHAPTER FOUR

MISTER LEWIS DESPAIRS

While we all waited for the Luas outside Heuston Station, Shane pointed to the sky. 'See, Milo?' he said. 'No rain. It must mean that Dublin is nearer to the equator.'

Well, I didn't argue with that. Sometimes Shane comes out with very weird information that he and Big Ella read from old books she buys from the charity shop. Other times, he makes up his own information, and I never can tell which is which so I just nod.

'So this is Dublin.'

I jumped when Mister Lewis whispered in my ear.

'I wish you wouldn't do that,' I said.

'Do what, Milo?'

'Creep up like that when you're invisible. You could pat my shoulder first. Then I wouldn't freak out.'

'You know my hands just go through things, Milo,' he sniffed.

'Sorry, I forgot,' I said. 'Maybe if you just gave a cough I wouldn't jump, OK?'

'I'll try to remember that, lad,' he said. 'I'm just so excited, you see. The last time I saw Dublin was in 1886.'

'Wow!' put in Shane. 'I've never been to Dublin at all.'

'I've been here before,' I said. 'It's just an ordinary place really.'

'Show off,' said Shane, thumping my arm. 'Last time you were here was when you were seven and all you remembered was Santa in a big shop. And you puked ice cream on his boots.'

We could hear Mister Lewis chuckling.

Then someone shouted out 'Luas!' followed by more shouts along the platform from other kids, 'Luas!' Here's the Luas!' 'The Luas is coming!'

Mister Lewis went into a tizzy, 'What's happening, Milo? Look at me, lad. Am I beginning to show myself? Can you see my chin? My ears? Oh dear, where shall I hide?'

'No,' I said, laughing. 'It's the tram coming – it's called the Luas.'

'Ah,' he sighed. 'That's a relief. And indeed an honour,' he added. 'It must be called after some relation of mine.'

I hadn't the heart to tell him that the word meant 'speed'.

When we all squashed into the Luas, we looked through the crowd of passengers, to see if Wedge and Crunch were going to elbow their way towards us.

'It's OK,' whispered Shane, standing on his tippy toes and looking over the crammed bodies. 'I see them, Milo. They're stuck between Miss Lee and Mister Brody. No worries. We're safe.'

'For now,' I muttered.

It wasn't a long walk to Dublinia when we got off the Luas. Mister Lewis, wafting invisibly beside me, went on and on into my ears about the bridges over the Liffey and the architecture of high buildings that weren't there in his time. Shane went on and on about the chip shops and restaurants, and the delicious smells.

CHAPTER FIVE

DUBLINIA

We were all herded through the door of Dublinia, everyone chattering and whooping. Shane and I felt the buzz from the first step inside. I looked around the crowded foyer for Wedge and Crunch. Knowing that they had no interest in the museum, I secretly hoped they'd scarper into the city. I spotted them near the entrance. Mister Brody was keeping his big glasses focused on them all the time while Miss Lee and the principal talked to the ticket people.

'All the chambers are small,' Mister Brody announced, when we had all crowded into the reception area. 'So, move around in small groups and meet back at the foyer at three thirty. Myself, the principal and Miss Lee will always be nearby,' he added with a threatening sort of frown, which brought his eyebrows together like a hairy caterpillar slithering across his big forehead.

'Chambers?' said Shane. 'Wow! That's,

like, overdoing the whole medieval thing for real. I'm glad I didn't drink my apple juice.'

'What do you mean?' I asked.

'Chambers,' he replied. 'You know – potties. For weeing into.'

'What kind of bug has got into your head, Shane?' I said.

'You're thinking of chamber pots, Shane,' the still-invisible Mister Lewis whispered. 'Old-fashioned lavatories. But chambers also mean rooms, lad.'

'Ha,' Shane grinned when the penny dropped. 'I knew that already,' he fibbed. 'I was just messing.'

'Yeah, right,' I laughed. 'Just make sure not to wee in any of *those* chambers.'

Neither of them laughed. Sometimes

my jokes are lost on people.

'All right, everyone,' Miss Lee called out. 'Line up.'

We were all given free, silver-painted Viking helmets as we went through to the museum.

'All part of the deal.' Miss Lee smiled, putting on her own helmet.

'This just gets better, Milo,' Shane whispered excitedly, as he pushed his helmet right down on his ears, making them stick right out.

I was sort of surprised when Mister Lewis came wafting invisibly around the exhibits with us.

'What about your three guys who've been stuck here?' I asked. 'Shouldn't you check them out, Mister Lewis?'

'I'm not quite sure where they are, or even what they look like,' he replied. 'All I know is that they've been trapped in this ancient square of land for centuries.'

'So, we don't know what we're looking for?' I said. 'They could look like any of the staff here who are dressed up in medieval gear?'

'That's it – more or less. How was I to know there would be staff dressed up in ancient outfits? All I was told was that these three unfortunates somehow got stuck here.'

'Is there someone you could ask, Mister Lewis?' said Shane.

'I don't think I could whisper into someone's ear and ask if they know of any lost warriors, Shane,' said Mister Lewis.

He sighed and sat on an ancient chair – I knew he was there when I saw the dust rise. He was tired and disheartened, sighing like my grandfather did when his cat, Sheba, went missing one Christmas (I found her sleeping on the donkey in the church crib).

'Never mind, Mister Lewis,' I said. 'We'll find them somehow. Let's go.'

So we started on our tour of all the 'ancient' interiors. We looked intently at totally realistic dead bodies piled in carts; people with their hands and legs locked in stocks; others standing up, their eyes almost following you. I couldn't see Mister Lewis, but I knew from his noisy sighs and groans that he was fast running out of optimism – as were me and Shane. We went into a hut where some wax models were sleeping on straw in small, wooden beds. Shane flopped down on the end of one of the beds and took one of Big Ella's sandwiches out of his bag.

'I'm pooped,' he said. 'I'm sick of looking at dummies – even if they are realistic. Anyone want an egg and crisps sandwich, with Big Ella's homemade mayonnaise? How about you, Mister Lewis, wherever you're sitting?'

And that's when one of the sleepers' eyes flicked open.

CHAPTER SIX

CONFUSED WARRIORS

'Mister Lewis!' exclaimed the man, his eyes swivelling around to Shane who had half a sandwich stuck in his mouth. 'Are you Mister Lewis?' the man asked in a shaky voice. Well, so would you feel shaky if you thought the man who'd come to save you was a stout kid with a half a sandwich stuck in his gob.

'I'm over here,' Mister Lewis said excitedly.

'I think you need to show yourself, Mister Lewis,' I whispered when I saw three pairs of eyes focused on me as the other two guys sat up too.

It was just unfortunate that the very moment all three warriors and Mister Lewis appeared together was also the moment Wedge and Crunch chose to stick their heads in the doorway of the hut.

'Hey,' Crunch laughed. 'You having a picnic with dummies, Shane?'

'Aww,' put in Wedge. 'Wouldn't it be better to share with live people? Come on, share.'

Mister Lewis and the warriors stayed absolutely still as Wedge and Crunch snatched the sandwiches from Shane. I confess I was annoyed when two ordinary, live people, who peered in, tut-tutted and moved on. Cowards, I thought, until I realised that I wasn't exactly helping my best friend either

'Do something,' I hissed at Mister Lewis. He didn't even blink, just sat glassy-eyed like a wax dummy.

We put up a bit of a fight, me and Shane, but the two scumbags took the grub and ran.

'Why didn't any of you do something?'

I asked.

'And have the whole staff rushing in and seeing these men sitting up and alive?' answered Mister Lewis. 'Try explaining that. Anyway, it's more important that we get these chaps out of here. If you give two of them your Viking helmets, they might just look like enthusiastic visitors in costume. Now, you two peep out and keep watch for staff, while I get Olaf, Gunnar and Alfred to make their beds look as if there's someone sleeping under the covers.'

Shane and I stood at the doorway to act as lookouts. Whenever people came along to look in, Shane began to cough, like he was about to vomit, so people hurried past quickly. I so wanted to say he had the plague like the dummies of dead people in a cart outside, but that might have caused a fuss. I mean, if someone shouted 'plague' in a realistic place like this, there would be a huge commotion, and Shane and I, plus Mister Lewis and the resurrected warriors, would cause a right old stir.

'Your helmets,' hissed Mister Lewis. 'Give them your helmets, lads.'

'Will we get them back?' asked Shane.

'Maybe,' said Mister Lewis. 'Probably,' he went on when he saw Shane's mouth go down. 'All right, everyone,' he said. 'Time to go. Just look natural.'

Natural? When I looked at the three warriors, two of them with cardboard Viking helmets, and Mister Lewis looking anything but natural, with his waxy face, high hat and long coat, I shook my head. This was pure mad.

CHAPTER SEVEN

MISTER LEWIS LEADS ON

Mister Lewis decided to stay visible. 'I can't have these chaps getting jittery if they can't see me,' he whispered.

'Will they be coming to the mock

battle with us?' I asked.

'Indeed, Milo,' he said, tapping his nose. 'I shall have a word with your nice Miss Lee.'

'You're going to talk to her like that?'

'Like what, Milo?'

'Well, no offence, Mister Lewis,' I whispered. 'But aren't your clothes a bit peculiar?'

'Look around you, lad,' he said, nodding towards the staff going around in their medieval costumes. 'I don't think anyone will query a different sort of ancient clothing.'

So off we went to wander, all six of us, through the museum, me and Shane leading. Sure enough, nobody took any notice of Olaf, Gunnar and Alfred –

except for some girls who wanted their autographs. Mister Lewis explained that the warriors weren't allowed as they had to focus on playing their ancient part. There was nearly a catastrophe when one of the girls then decided to ask Mister Lewis for his autograph.

'Your scruffy hat and makeup are dead creepy, mister,' she said, holding out her pen and notebook.

That was the first time I ever saw Mister Lewis nervous. This could be tricky, as his hands would go through the pen.

It was Shane who saved the situation.

'Hey girls,' he said, walking towards them. 'These guys are all my friends, I'll sign for them.'

The girls took one look at his jammy mouth and squealed with laughter as they ran away.

'You know, Milo,' Shane said as he looked after them, 'I think they liked me.'

'Perhaps you boys should go well ahead of us,' said Mister Lewis. 'It might seem strange if we're all together.'

Good idea, I thought.

'Are you sure you don't need me to chase away people who start asking questions?' asked Shane, flexing his muscles.

'I think we'll manage, Shane,' said Mister Lewis.

It was a relief really to be on our own. It was getting a bit tense, looking out for three ancient warriors and a spook. I mean, they seemed to be nice guys, those warriors, and Mister Lewis is a great pal, but now we could see more of the museum without worrying about dead people. Well, I know the warriors weren't *exactly* 'dead' but they were pretty darned old. We stopped at a small cabin where a medieval man was sitting on an ancient toilet.

'Hey, Milo,' said Shane. 'It says here that they used moss to wipe their bottoms. How gross is that?!'

'Better than the cheap loo paper in school,' I said with a laugh. 'Maybe we should try collecting moss ...' I broke off when Wedge and Crunch appeared behind us.

'Well, well,' said Wedge. 'If it isn't the deadly duo hanging about in an ancient loo.'

CHAPTER EIGHT

THE STOCKS

Our arch enemies put their arms around us, like we were all cool guys together as they steered us around the exhibits. We passed some of our classmates, here and there, but they weren't going to ask any questions.

Not to Wedge and Crunch. We did see the principal, Mrs Riley, looking up the nostrils of a slave trader, but we'd probably be called cowardly snitches forever after if we ran to her.

'Would you like to sit down, guys?' asked Wedge.

'Yes,' I said, thinking this would give us time for Mister Lewis and the warriors to catch up with us.

'You see, we've been through this whole place,' said Wedge.

'Yeah,' piped Crunch. 'The whole place.'

'And we know where the best seats are.' Wedge laughed. 'And here we are. Ever heard of stocks?' he asked, when we came to a deep corner with one of those ancient punishment things with holes for hands and feet. They both glanced around to see if anyone was coming, then forced me and Shane into the stocks, before we could even catch our breath.

'Move and I'll punch you,' hissed Wedge. 'Quick, Crunch, Gimme the string, before someone comes.'

'Ah, there's a much better way than that, chaps,' said a familiar voice.

'Who said that?' asked Crunch, looking around nervously.

'That would be me, young man,' replied Mister Lewis as he caught up.

'It's OK,' said Wedge, tightening the string. 'It's just an old guy.'

'And some other friends,' added

Mister Lewis, 'Come along, chaps,' he called out.

The three warriors came along, two of them proudly wearing our cardboard helmets, their swords dangling from their hips.

'We're not doing anything,' said Crunch. 'Just a bit of fun.'

'Oh,' said Mister Lewis. 'We love fun. Go ahead, my friends.'

Shane and I took our cue, and while Crunch and Wedge were distracted, we hopped up out of the stocks.

Olaf, Gunnar and Alfred seemed to be well acquainted with stocks as they pushed Wedge and Crunch on to the seat and expertly began to lock them in with the actual old locks. But my knees turned to jelly when Shane nudged me. There were voices from behind and a group of people and kids came towards us. How would we cope with this?

'Help!' cried Crunch. 'Save us! They're locking us in!'

'We're in right trouble now,' whispered Shane. 'Should we do a runner, Milo?'

I was tempted, but when I saw Mister Lewis's calm face I knew we were OK.

Mister Lewis turned towards the group and doffed his hat. 'You're just in time for a demonstration of how the stocks work, dear people,' he said.

'He's lying!' screeched Wedge. 'That man is spooky!'

'Help us, please!' shouted Crunch, as the last lock clicked into place.

'Wow!' said a man with shorts and hairy legs. 'This is real drama. Those prisoners sound so genuine.'

Olaf, Gunnar and Alfred stood up and bowed to great applause from the people who'd now been joined by another group.

'Great show,' said a woman. 'So realistic.'

Everyone agreed it had been a good show before moving on.

'Wait!' pleaded Wedge. 'Get some of the staff. PLEASE!'

'Those guys,' the man in shorts was saying. 'They're so convincing. Should be on the stage.'

'That was fun, Master Lewis,' said Olaf, the tallest of the three warriors.

'Could we do it again?'

'If only we had known, we could have been doing this ourselves instead of just lying about on hard beds,' said Gunnar. 'Could we stay on and do it again for other people?'

'Afraid not,' said Mister Lewis. 'We need to get back and be on time for the journey to Clontarf.

'What about those two?' I asked, nodding back towards the snivelling Wedge and Crunch, still pleading loudly.

'Oh, I'm sure one of the teachers will spot them soon enough,' said Mister Lewis with a big grin.

CHAPTER NINE

WILLIE JONES'S CHALLENGE

There were two open-top buses waiting for us when we went outside. Mister Lewis had taken off his tall hat and was speaking to the principal, Mrs

Riley, and Miss Lee, and pointing to the three long-haired warriors. I shut my eyes when the principal tried to shake hands with Mister Lewis, but the spook pretended not to notice and introduced the warriors, and they shook hands.

'They've missed their transport to the battle,' Mister Lewis fibbed. 'I'm in charge of getting them there.'

'No problem, my dear man,' gushed the principal. 'We shall certainly fit you in.'

Miss Lee spotted me and Shane and called us over. 'Boys,' she said, 'will you take these four gentlemen to the top of the bus before the mad scramble for seats?'

'Nice one, Milo,' whispered Shane,

clutching his bag. 'We get to have the best seats.'

At first, the warriors were a bit doubtful about getting into the bus, but Mister Lewis explained that they were many centuries from their own time and there had been lots of changes in the world.

'Just do as I did when I came to this century,' he said to them.

'And what was that?' asked Shane.

'Go with the flow,' said Mister Lewis.

'Go with the flow?' the puzzled warriors said to one another.

'Like, just don't freak out at whatever you see,' put in Shane.

'Freak out?' said Olaf.

'Just enjoy it,' I said. How could you

possibly even begin to tell people from 1014 about all the stuff that even my mum can't handle, like i-pods, e-books, Kindles, laptops, and dishwashers.

The warriors panicked when the bus moved off, but settled down after a few minutes when Mister Lewis pointed to the rest of us sitting down.

Everything went fine until we were passing along the river Liffey and Gunnar spotted the Viking Experience water bus. It was full of people and kids, wearing Viking helmets and waving cardboard swords, All three warriors jumped up, waving their seriously real swords. Gunnar tightened his belt over his ample tummy and looked like he was getting ready to jump off the top deck of the bus! The warriors shouted and hollered all kinds of words none of us had ever heard before.

The people on the riverbus responded with loud laughter and make-believe warrior whoops. Our classmates behind us joined in with mock battle-cries. It was all getting out of hand. Luckily, the bus moved faster, and I sighed with relief when we reached O'Connell Street.

'Whew,' I whispered to Shane. 'That was close.'

'Not over yet, Milo,' he said, as Olaf, Gunnar and Alfred stood up again, shouting at cars this time. They bowed to the high spike in the middle of the street and, when the bus stopped at the lights, they roared at a big cinema poster of a woman wielding a gun and a sword. The kids behind us thought this was hilarious and joined in the act again.

Mister Lewis was mortified. 'I wish I'd gone invisible,' he groaned. 'I wish I was at home in my cosy room in the castle.'

The trio finally settled down when the principal came upstairs and told them they were taking their role far too seriously. 'Behave like gentlemen.'

'What is "gentlemen"?' whispered Olaf when she'd left.

'Nerds in suits with haircuts, matching socks and shiny shoes,' said Shane. 'Like Mister Brody,' he added, pointing down the aisle to Mister Brody who had managed to sleep throughout the commotion, being well used to lots of shouting in his class. Though he did wake up startled when Gunnar, Alfred and Olaf went back and bowed to him.

'Greetings, gentleman,' said Olaf.

'Eh?' said Mister Brody, his forehead wrinkling with puzzlement.

'Eh,' said Gunnar and Alfred.

Later on, when Mister Brody went downstairs, Willie Jones wandered up to us. 'Hey lads, how come you two got to sit behind the actors?' he asked, sucking a lump of Dublin rock so much that the top had shaped into a sharp pink and white point.

'Because we saved them,' replied

Shane, who never thinks before he speaks.

'Saved them from what?' asked Willie, taking another slurp of rock.

'Emm,' began Shane, looking pathetically at me for an answer.

'They got locked' was the best I could come up with.

'Locked!' exclaimed Willy. 'You mean drunk?'

'No, they were locked in,' muttered Shane.

'Locked in where?'

'In a hole,' I said, knowing that I sounded like a croaking frog because I was trying to focus on my brain and mouth at the same time, and it wasn't working very well.

'You're a right daft pair of nutters,' Willy said, with a laugh. 'Let's say hello to the actors,' he went on, moving to the seat in front of us.

'No! Leave them alone,' I yelped. 'They're – eh – tired.'

'What do you know?' said Willie. 'You're not in charge.'

'What'll we do now, Milo?' asked Shane.

'Just stay calm,' I said, clenching my hands with panic and hoping the warriors wouldn't think Willy was another sort of Wedge and Crunch and throw him over the side of the bus.

'Hey,' Willy began, 'that's a mighty sword you have there, Mister, Is it real?'

'What else could it be, boy?' said Olaf.

'Ha,' grinned Willy, posing like a swordfighter. 'So, Mister Smartypants, I'll run you through with my dagger.' He laughed, holding out the sharp point of his Dublin rock.

With a quick swoop of his sword, Olaf swished the stick of rock in two. Everyone froze. And then the commotion began. Mister Lewis jumped up and swore at Olaf; everyone else was too shocked to move.

Except Willy. 'Cool, Mister,' he said, picking up the topped stick of rock. 'Here,' he added, as he held the rock out to Olaf. 'You can have that if you'll let me hold your sword for a second. Huh?'

'Indeed, boy,' said Olaf, shoving the

pink rock into his mouth.

Within seconds, Mrs Riley stomped up the stairs. 'What's all the commotion up here?' she bellowed.

That's when Willy swung the sword, just as Olaf had shown him.

Mrs Riley slid gracefully to the floor, asking gently for smelling salts.

CHAPTER TEN

BULLIES AND BUNS

There were hundreds of people scattered around the field where the battle was about to take place.

'Wow, this is awesome,' said Shane,

looking around the packed battlefield.
'Look at all the tents.'

'You're looking the wrong way,' I said,
pointing to the tents with decorative
flags flying on the other side.

'No, I'm not,' he said. 'I can smell the
burgers from the tents on this side.'

'Don't you ever think of anything
else?' I laughed. 'Come on, we'd best
keep up with the school or we might
find ourselves stuck in a battle.'

'There's Mister Lewis and the
warriors,' said Shane, pointing again
towards the food tents. 'Let's go over to
them.'

So we made our way there, keeping
clear of Mrs Riley who was sitting on
a deck chair taking a glass of something

yellow from Miss Lee for her nerves.

Sure enough, Mister Lewis seemed to be arguing with a stout woman, her big arms folded over her chest. Olaf, Alfred and Gunnar were staring bug-eyed at the array of goodies.

'But these three warriors haven't eaten for – eh – a long time,' Mister Lewis was saying.

'Olaf had sticky rock,' began Gunnar, before Olaf stamped on his toe.

'I don't care if they haven't eaten for a week,' the woman retorted. 'D'ye think I spent last night up to me elbows in flour and eggs to make freebie cakes and buns for big lumps of scruffy lads dressed up like them? Just because you lot are part of the pageant doesn't mean you can scrounge. Go on, off with ye.'

Mister Lewis looked miserable. 'Our warriors have smelled the food,' he whispered miserably to me and Shane. 'And I'm afraid they'll create a scene with this lady. The only money I have is a farthing from the eighteen hundreds.'

'Excuse me, Missus,' put in Shane.

I groaned because I knew what he was going to say next. 'These are *real* warriors from the eleventh century ...'

'Yeah,' said the woman. 'And I'm Queen Victoria.'

'Wait,' went on Shane, digging into his pocket and fishing out a five euro note. 'Will this be enough?'

Naturally, I had to follow his example and take out three euro coins – not that

I'm mean, you understand, but I'd read a book about self-preservation in the wilds and felt it was proper to hang on to the last few euro for safety.

The woman sniffed. 'I suppose so,' she said, then glared at Mister Lewis and the warriors. 'Ye should be ashamed of yerselves,' she muttered, as she shovelled buns into a paper bag. 'Letting two young fellas pay for ye.'

Olaf leaned towards her, 'Madam,' he began, 'my two warriors and I have been buried ...'

'In mud,' put in Mister Lewis very quickly. 'For the festival, you see.'

'Should have stayed buried,' she sniffed. 'Here, young fellas,' she said, handing Shane and me a big squishy bun each. 'That's for your generosity.'

We beamed like lighthouses as we followed Mister Lewis and the warriors, who were already stuffing their cheeks with buns and moaning with delight.

'Look at them, Shane,' I said. 'They must have had nothing to eat for centuries.'

'Nor me,' said Shane, licking the cream from his free bun. 'I've had nothing to eat since mmm.' He looked at his watch. 'Three whole hours. Come on,' he went on. 'We can't rush with these totally scrumptious buns, Milo. You have to savour good food and this is as good as food gets.'

Well, he had a point there. In spite of the crowds, we'd have no problem finding Mister Lewis with his long coat and crooked hat, accompanying three scruffy warriors, two of them wearing cardboard helmets.

'Ah, no worries,' Shane sighed, leaning against a tree and taking a delighted bite off the top of his bun. 'Bliss.' That is until we heard two familiar voices. Yes – Wedge and Crunch.

'Well, well. If it isn't our good friends slurping fine buns,' said Crunch, looking around for Mister Lewis and the warriors.

'Won't you share it with your good friends, me and Wedge?' he asked bravely when he saw we were on our own.

'No way,' I retorted. 'Get lost.'

'Or we'll get our warrior pals to deal with you,' added Shane.

'Yeah, right,' said Crunch, looking around. 'They'll be over at the battlefield getting ready for the fight. So, hand over those buns NOW!'

I looked around desperately. There was definitely no sign of them or Mister Lewis.

'OLAF!' I shouted.

Wedge laughed. 'What's an Olaf? You mean a *loaf*?'

'Nice one, Wedge,' said Crunch. 'Dead clever that. Come on guys, time to hand over.'

'No way!' shouted Shane, holding up his half-eaten bun.

I went over to stand with him,

well, sort of behind him. I knew we hadn't a chance.

'OOLAAAAF!' I shouted again.

Then, just as Wedge was about to grab my bun, there was a loud roar, like a bull with a headache, as Olaf thrust his way through the crowd, followed by Gunnar and Alfred. People gathered round us as Olaf and Alfred threw Wedge and Crunch up in the air, like a couple of floppy scarecrows, and tossed them to one another like a game of 'catch'.

'Help us,' shouted Crunch. The more they cried out, the more they were thrown up and the more the crowd laughed and clapped. And we ate our buns.

'How did you hear me through all the noisy crowds and loud music?' I asked Olaf when they let Wedge and Crunch run as far away as possible.

He pointed to his ears. 'We've lived for hundreds of years under Dublin,' he said. 'Our ears have tuned into all sorts of voices and noises.'

'Cool,' said Shane. 'Could you train me to do that?'

On our way towards the battlefield, we met Mister Lewis, puffing and panting as he floated towards us.

'I shouldn't have eaten *two* whole buns,' he wheezed. 'They nearly killed me. Oops,' he went on, 'I forgot. I'm already dead.'

We all laughed.

CHAPTER ELEVEN

TIME FOR BATTLE

Crowds were beginning to gather at the battlefield.

'We won't get to see anything,' wailed Shane. 'There's loads of people in front of us.'

'Not for long, lad,' said Olaf. 'Follow us.'

Then he, Gunnar and Alfred pushed through the crowd and got us right up to the barrier, ignoring the shouts and thumps from the people who'd probably lined up for hours.

'This is where we must fight with Brian Boru,' Gunnar snarled, getting into battle mode.

'Yeah,' a man shouted. 'Me too!'

Everyone laughed, especially when Alfred asked him had he seen Brian Boru.

'Sure,' the man replied. 'He's just having his hair and makeup done.'

'Maybe you'll lend him your toy helmet,' someone else called out.

'That's a joke,' whispered Mister Lewis when he saw Gunnar reach for his sword.

'Joke?' said Alfred. 'What is "a joke"?'

'It's a laugh,' I explained.

'Ah, Brian Boru is laughing?' put in Gunnar. 'I have never seen him laugh.'

'Oh dear,' sighed Mister Lewis in my ear. 'How can I tell them that this is just a pageant?'

'So, why have you brought them here, Mister Lewis?' I asked.

He took a deep breath. 'Hope, Milo,' he whispered. 'This is the exact day of the battle and this is the exact place. Most of all,' he went on, 'it is the thousandth year, which is very significant for time changes. I've studied the movements of the sun and the moon, but my fear is that the time of the real battle was earlier. I hope all will knit together. So, boys, it *is* indeed all down to hope.'

Shane and I looked at one another, neither of us understanding what he was talking about.

'Hope?' I said, as it was the only word that stuck in my mind. 'We're just depending on hope?'

'Trust me, lad,' he replied.

The fact that he had his fingers crossed when he said that made my heart thump like a road drill. If this didn't work after all, how would I explain to Mum and Dad that me and Shane had to go and visit three old fellas in prison? Olaf, Gunnar and Alfred were bound to be arrested if they attacked the actors in the pageant. I couldn't imagine hot-headed Alfred in handcuffs!

'Couldn't you just persuade them to leave and go and live in the castle with you?' I asked Mister Lewis.

He shook his head so strongly that part of his nose came loose. ''Fraid not, lads. Events have been set in motion now. And, anyway, I couldn't have them wandering around when tourists come to see our wonderful castle?' he gasped, tightening his nose. 'Not likely. It's hard enough to do my invisible ooohhhs and aaaghs, without having that three jumping out with their swords at unfortunate visitors.'

'That's all right,' put in Shane who had just joined us. 'Big Ella would be delighted to put them up. They could help with her paintings.'

'Good idea,' I cheered, imagining a happy ending. Big Ella paints big, splashy paintings on canvas. 'The warriors could pose for her and maybe do the washing up and gardening as well.'

Whew, that was a plan.

Before we could sink into more thoughts of what really might or might not happen, two buglers sounded their horns.

'Ladies and gentlemen,' one of them called out. 'Prepare ye for the great Battle of Clontarf.'

There was loud cheering. Then, as the warriors came into the field from different sides, there was silence.

'Ho!' exclaimed Olaf. 'What mess is this? These are no warriors that we know.'

'Ragged peasants,' added Gunnar. There should be thousands of warriors on each side. This is farcical, Mister Lewis. Why have you brought us here? Where is Brian Boru?'

'Let us go and show them how real warriors battle,' shouted Alfred.

'Shush,' whispered Mister Lewis. 'People are looking. We'll be kicked out if you don't behave yourselves. Your time is soon. And put those swords away until it's time to go. You've nearly cost me an ear.'

So we watched the 'battle' as it progressed – the onlookers shouting loudly for any side because nobody knew who was fighting whom. Helmets rolled along the ground;

homemade shields were smashed; real shields clashed and, above all there were the shouts and screams. The noise was so loud that I didn't hear what Mister Lewis said to Olaf, Gunnar and Alfred as they unsheathed their swords and handed Shane and me our Viking helmets.

'Thank you, boys,' said Olaf.

'No problem,' I said. 'It's been a blast hanging out with you guys.'

'A blast, indeed, as you say in these strange times,' added in Alfred, putting his hand on my shoulder.

'Any moment now,' Mister Lewis was saying, looking up at the sun. Our three friends stood up straight and mighty, their faces serious. They were no longer the lost souls who couldn't understand our century. They were true warriors getting ready for battle.

'They're never going to fight that lot!' hissed Shane. 'Tell them, Mister Lewis,' he added, his voice trembling. 'They're just ordinary guys out there!'

'Hush,' said Mister Lewis, still looking upwards, shielding his eyes with his hand. Then the strangest thing happened. Right in front of us a wobbly image appeared, like it was a film mixed in with the present-day battle. Shane and I gasped at the thousands of clashing warriors that shimmered in front of us.

'Look!' someone behind us called out. 'Isn't that real clever?! Someone is superimposing an actual film on the battle. Wow!'

'It's time!' said Mister Lewis turning to the warriors.

'Aye,' said Gunnar, his eyes blazing. 'There's Brian Boru and his army.'

'And there's Sigtrygg leading his Dublin Vikings to battle,' said Alfred, pointing to a whole army marching from the other side of the image.

'Go now,' said Mister Lewis. 'And God speed.'

The three warriors patted Shane and me on the shoulders and, with a ferocious battle-cry, they jumped over the rope and headed straight out into the real Battle of Clontarf. We saw them pitch in with their comrades. For one brief moment, Olaf paused and glanced over at us before giving a loud roar and running into battle. Then they all disappeared.

'Ah, so,' sighed Mister Lewis. 'They've got back to the battle. All is well.'

'Hey!' people behind us called out. 'The film is gone!'

'Huh!' moaned another. 'It was probably some no brainer amateur trying out his new video.'

'Tell me something, Mister Lewis,' I said later as we sat in the train. 'How come their hands can lift things and yours can't?'

He looked at his hands for a moment. 'Well,' he said, 'it's simple really. I'm dead, but they weren't. They were simply lost underground, suspended in time, until they made their way to Dublinia.'

'So, me and Milo are real, true heroes!' put in Shane. 'Cool.'

I figured he was right. 'Dead cool, Shane,' I said, giving him a high five.

CHAPTER TWELVE

THE LAST STAND

Miss Lee was handing back the essays we had to write about our visit to Dublinia and the Pageant of the Battle of Clontarf. I chose Dublinia because I felt that there was no way I could even begin to explain the events at Clontarf, without getting myself into a knot trying to avoid the incredible parts that would have me classed as an A1 looney.

However, Shane had no such qualms. Miss Lee kept his essay until last.

'Well, Shane,' she said. 'Your essay is the most creative essay I've read since I became a teacher.'

At first Shane's mouth dropped to his chest with surprise. 'Are you talking about me, Miss?' he asked.

'Of course I am,' Miss Lee smiled.

'What does "creative" mean? asked Willie Jones.

'It means the ability to make up stories in your mind,' Miss Lee began.

'Make up stories?' Shane spluttered. 'I didn't make up any stories, Miss.

Everything I wrote is absolutely true!'

'Really, Shane?' Miss Lee asked. 'You had buns with real warriors and a ghost with a high hat? And you saw part of the actual real Battle of Clontarf in 1014?'

'Yes, Miss.'

'And you gave your Viking helmet to a warrior?'

'I did,' responded Shane. 'In fact I have it here,' he went on, taking the tatty cardboard helmet from his bag and holding it up.

The class erupted with laughter.

'Look, Miss,' said Shane, pointing to a black mark on the helmet. 'That's because of a dirty thumb mark from Alfred when he was buried for hundreds of years under Dublin.'

'That's one of the helmets we were given in Dublinia,' piped up Willy Jones. 'You're a right chancer, Shane.'

'Shush, you lot,' said Miss Lee when the hoots of laughter got out of hand.

'I'm telling the truth, Miss,' went on Shane. 'Ask Milo.'

I groaned and slipped down under my desk.

Luckily, the bell went for hometime.

I dragged Shane into the cloakroom.

'We'll wait here until the coast is clear,' I whispered. 'We'll be jeered if we go out now.'

'Not me,' said Shane, puffing out his big chest. 'I'll clobber anyone ...'

'Think, Shane,' I said.

'Yeah, you're right,' he mumbled.

When it was all clear, we grabbed our bikes and took off like greased greyhounds on skates. I so wanted to yell at Shane for including me in his answer to Miss Lee, but, hey, he's my best mate.

We stopped at the castle to say hello to Mister Lewis, but he wasn't showing himself.

'Probably having a nap,' I said.

'Oh, no,' groaned Shane. 'Look who's coming through the arch!'

It was Wedge and Crunch, and there was no way they were simply coming to pay for a tour of the castle.

'Aha,' laughed Wedge. 'Gotcha. We followed you.'

'Because we owe you,' sneered Crunch.

'Owe us for what?' I croaked, looking about, hoping for a tourist or two to come through the arch.

'For having those weird guys throwing us about at the Battle of Clontarf thingy for one,' said Wedge.

'And for having us stuck in the stocks in Dublinia, for another,' added Crunch. 'So it's your turn to squeal for mercy.'

'First of all, we'll take your money,' said Wedge. 'We wouldn't want it damaged or lost when we rough you up.'

Shane looked at me. His face went from its normal coffee colour to light beige. As for me, I clenched my fists, but I knew we hadn't a hope against these two — especially after the trouble we'd got them into.

'OK, fat boy,' Wedge snarled. 'You usually have cash in your pockets. Hand it over, NOW!' he bellowed.

'And you too, shrimp,' put in Crunch, stepping towards me.

'Hello boyssss' came a hissing sound from behind Wedge. He turned around.

'Who said that?' he croaked.

'That would be me,' whispered the voice, now behind Crunch.

'You two dissing me and Crunch?' said Wedge with a frown.

Shane and I shrugged our shoulders.

'Not us, Maybe you're hallucinating,' I said bravely, now that I knew Mister Lewis was on board.

'Liars,' shouted Wedge.

'Ooooohhh noooo' came the voice again, this time right into Crunch's ear.

That finished him. He took off like a rocket, yelling all the way to the arch.

Wedge waited for half a second and scarpered too.

'That went rather well,' said Mister Lewis. 'Now, let's go to the castle garden and chat about our great trip. Do you have any chocolate, Shane?'

I laughed. Shane always has a stash of goodies in his pockets.

READ MORE MILO ADVENTURES FROM

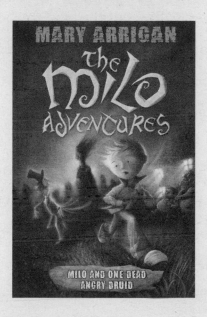

MILO AND ONE DEAD ANGRY DRUID

On that Tuesday, when our teacher Miss Lee said that we were all to bring something old to school and talk about it, Shane stood up and said that he'd bring something totally amazing. The class laughed and said, 'Oh, yeah?'

And he said, 'Sure. Just you wait.'

So everyone laughed again. Well,

everyone except me. That was because Shane was my best mate. He lived at the end of my road with his gran, Big Ella, who painted big splashy paintings in mad colours. She said Ireland needed sunshiny colours on account of all the grey rain.

Shane's clothes were way too small for him because he was a bit of a roly-poly, addicted to jammy donuts, squishy marshmallows and crisps. And yes, he did munch them all together.

Whenever anyone sniggered at his wobbly tummy, he'd just say that his chest had slipped a bit – like Obelix in my dad's old *Asterix* comics that Shane and I shared.

Nobody could make Shane angry. If his dark skin was pointed at by some idiot, he'd say he was 'well done' and not a 'half-baked porridge-face'. Everything was a laugh. Except if anyone made fun of his gran. That's when he'd roar like a bull and flatten them and then sit on them until they screamed. If they were smaller than him, that is.

Big Ella was the sort of person who made you feel glad to be with her. She was fun too, and I liked to visit her house because she was always either baking brilliant African lime cakes or painting big pictures, which she exhibited in the local art gallery.

Nobody knew what the pictures were about, not even if you looked sideways or stood on your head. So she didn't sell many, except maybe to someone who wanted to hide a damp wall or scare away intruders.

Sometimes Big Ella and Shane went away for days when she'd get a notion to paint some foggy mountain or windy lake. So, when they disappeared after the taking-something-old-to-school day, people just said what a nutter she was to take a young lad away from school. Nobody was worried. Except me. You see, I knew. And I was really scared.

BEYOND THE PORTAL

Milo's ghostly buddy, Mister Lewis, appears in the
town's ancient castle, but he's not alone. He's in
trouble and needs Milo's help.
Things get very complicated when Milo's teacher,
Miss Lee, accidentally wakes some raging chieftains
from long ago.
And then she disappears.

Mister Lewis takes Milo and Shane through
the castle time portal ... into a

MILO ADVENTURE

WORLD
BOOK
DAY
6 MARCH 2014

WORLD BOOK DAY fest

Want to **READ** more?

 your **LOCAL BOOKSHOP**

- Get some great recommendations for what to read next

- Meet your favourite authors & illustrators at brilliant events

- Discover books you never even knew existed!

 WWW.BOOKSELLERS.ORG.UK/ BOOKSHOPSEARCH

 your **LOCAL LIBRARY**

You can browse and borrow from a HUGE selection of books and get recommendations of what to read next from expert librarians—all for FREE! You can also discover libraries' wonderful children's and family reading activities—such as reading groups, author events and challenges (suc as www.msreadathon.ie).

 Visit **WWW.WORLDBOOKDAY.COM** to discover a whole *new* world of book

- Downloads and activities
- Cool games, trailers and videos
- Author events in your area
- News, competitions and new books —all in a **FREE** monthly email